THE END

My papa!

But, what I like **BEST** about my papa...

is that he's...

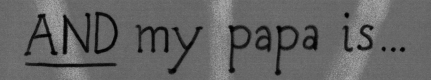

AND my papa is...

A HIDE-N-SEEK CHAMPION!

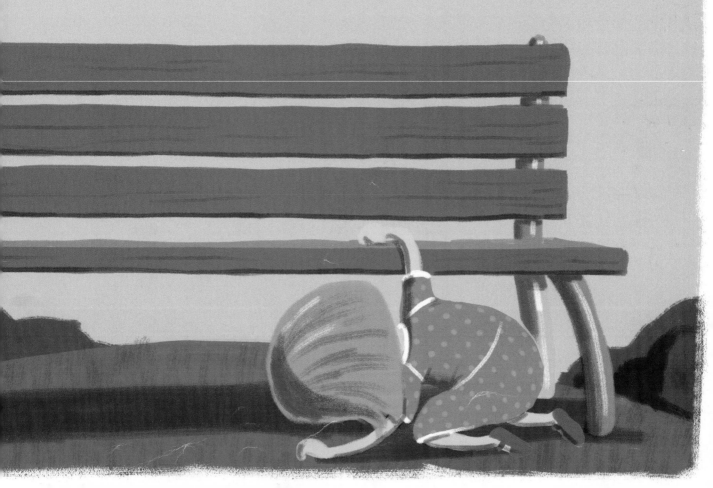

My papa is...

A MASTER CHEF!

My papa is...

A FIREFIGHTER!

AN ART COLLECTOR!

My papa is...

AN ASTRONAUT!

My papa is...

My papa is a lot of things...

MY PAPA IS A Princess

BY DOUG CENKO

For MY princess, Olive Rose.
-DC

Text copyright 2018 by Doug Cenko
Illustrations copyright 2018 by Doug Cenko

Published by blue manatee press, Cincinnati, Ohio.
blue manatee press and associated logo
are registered trademarks of Arete Ventures, LLC.

First Edition: September 2018.

Library of Congress Cataloging-In-Publication Data
My Papa Is a Princess / by Doug Cenko—1st ed.
Summary: Cuddle up with Dad for this sweet book about a father as seen through his
daughter's eyes. When Papa braids her hair, he's a hairdresser; when he hangs her drawings on
the wall, he's an art collector. But no matter what happens, he is always her papa, and that's the
most important thing of all!
ISBN-13 (hardcover): 978-1-936669-70-7
[Juvenile Fiction – Imagination & Play. 2. Juvenile Fiction – Family/Parents.]
Printed in the USA.

Artwork was created digitally.